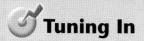

Tuning In

The Seven Continents can be read from [...] may be more appropriate to read sele[...] notes take account of this.

The front cover

Read the title.
What is a continent?
Can you name a continent?

Speaking and Listening?

What information do you expect to read about in this book?

The back cover

Read the blurb to find out if the information given in this book is what you expected.

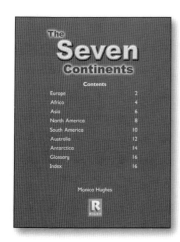

Contents

The list of contents gives the names of the continents.

Which ones did we know?

As we read this book, we are going to make a note of some of the facts.

Read pages 2 and 3

Purpose: to find out about the Vatican City.

Pause at page 3

What are three facts about Europe?

Which words would you expect to find in the glossary?

What do they mean?

Speaking and Listening

Which fact did you find the most interesting?

How can we write it down without copying the sentence?

EUROPE

In Europe you will find the Vatican City, the smallest country in the world. The Vatican has its own **government**, its own money and stamps and has the world's biggest church, St. Peter's Basilica.

*The Vatican City is found in the centre of Rome, the **capital** city of Italy.*

Many different animals live in Europe. Northern Europe is much colder than Southern Europe and is home to the reindeer.

*Reindeer dig through the snow to graze on **lichen**, which is also known as 'reindeer moss'.*

France is the largest country in Europe and Paris is its capital.

FACT BOX

The United Kingdom is found in Europe. It is made up of four countries, England, Northern Ireland, Scotland and Wales.

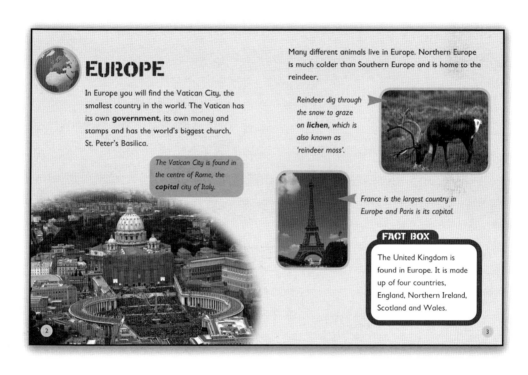

Read pages 4 and 5

Purpose: to read information about Africa.

Pause at page 5

Was there information about Africa that you knew already?

Was there information about Africa that surprised you?

Speaking and Listening

Which fact shall we make a note of?

How can we write it down without copying the sentence?

AFRICA

Africa is the warmest continent. Here you will find the largest desert in the world, the Sahara, which also has the world's highest sand dunes. The world's highest temperature (58 °C) was recorded in the Sahara. At night, the temperature can fall to below freezing.

The Sahara Desert gets its name from the Arabic word 'Sahra', meaning desert.

On this continent you will find the chimpanzee and gorilla, along with monkeys, zebras, giraffes and elephants.

*In many parts of Africa, the elephant is protected in National Parks. It is at danger from **poachers** who hunt it for its long tusks.*

There are many big cities and fine buildings in Africa.

FACT BOX

Africa is the second largest continent and has 54 different countries.

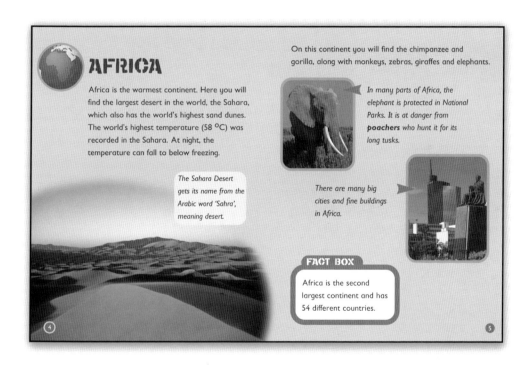

Read pages 6 and 7

Purpose: to read information about Asia.

Pause at page 7

What information is given about Mount Everest?

What is one fact that you did not know?

Speaking and Listening

What information did you find the most interesting?

How can we make a note of it without copying the sentence?

ASIA

Asia is where you will find the world's highest mountain, Mount Everest. The mountain is also known locally as 'goddess of the sky' and 'mother goddess of the universe'. Mount Everest is part of the **Himalayas**.

Many different animals live on this continent. Here you will find the small Indian elephant, tigers and rhinoceros.

No two tigers have the same pattern of stripes.

*Edmund Hilary and Tenzing Norgay were the first people to climb to the **summit** of Mount Everest in 1953.*

FACT BOX

Asia has the world's longest railway. It is 5,864 miles long!

The Great Wall of China is one of Asia's most famous sights.

Read pages 8 and 9

Purpose: to read information about North America.

Pause at page 9

Can you name a country that is part of North America?

What is special about Lake Superior?

Speaking and Listening

What information shall we make notes about?

NORTH AMERICA

In North America you will find the River Roe, the shortest river in the world, and Lake Superior, the largest **freshwater** lake in the world.

Bald Eagles, Polar Bears (the largest **carnivore** in the world) and smaller Grizzly Bears all live in North America.

The Bald Eagle builds the largest nest in the world.

Lake Superior is more than 300 miles long and more than 100 miles wide in places.

Alaska is the most northern part of North America. Very few people live here.

FACT BOX
There are 23 different countries in North America.

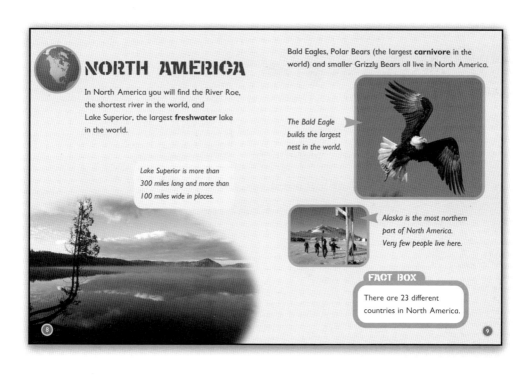

READ

Read pages 10 and 11

Purpose: to read information about South America.

PAUSE

Pause at page 11

Can you name a country that is part of South America?

Which fact did you find the most interesting?

Speaking and Listening

What information shall we make notes about?

SOUTH AMERICA

In South America you will find the Andes, the longest mountain chain in the world, and the Amazon, the largest rainforest in the world.

Brazil is the largest country in South America. Argentina is the second largest.

The Amazon River is 4000 miles long. It is one of the longest rivers in the world.

Argentina has many huge cattle ranches. Argentinean cowboys called 'gauchos' herd the cattle.

Sloths live in the Amazon rainforest.

FACT BOX

South America is twice the size of Europe.

READ

Read pages 12 and 13

Purpose: to find out what countries make up the Australasian continent.

PAUSE

Pause at page 13

Which words would you expect to find in the glossary?

What do they mean?

Speaking and Listening

Which fact do you find the most interesting?

How can we make a note of it without copying the sentence?

AUSTRALIA

Australia is both a continent and a country. It is where you will find the Great Barrier Reef, the longest **coral reef** in the world. It stretches for more than 1,000 miles and contains over 300 different kinds of coral.

Australia produces more than a quarter of the world's wool. There are many more sheep than there are people on this continent.

Australian farmers keep sheep and cattle on large farms called 'stations'.

Koala bears live in Australia. They get their name from an **Aboriginal** word meaning 'no drink'.

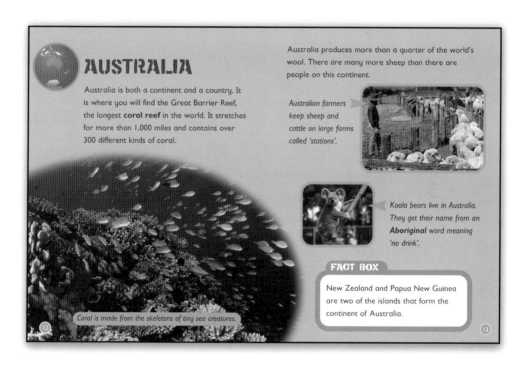

Coral is made from the skeletons of tiny sea creatures.

FACT BOX

New Zealand and Papua New Guinea are two of the islands that form the continent of Australia.

Read pages 14 and 15

Purpose: to find out about Antarctica.

Pause at page 15

What are three things you have found out about Antarctica?

Speaking and Listening

What information did you already know?

What information was new?

What information shall we make notes about?

ANTARCTICA

Antarctica is the coldest continent in the world, and it is here that you will find the largest piece of ice on Earth. In summer, the edges of the ice melt and break off into the sea to form icebergs. Icebergs then drift away from the continent.

Very few people live on this continent. The animals that do, like penguins and seals, live on fish from the sea.

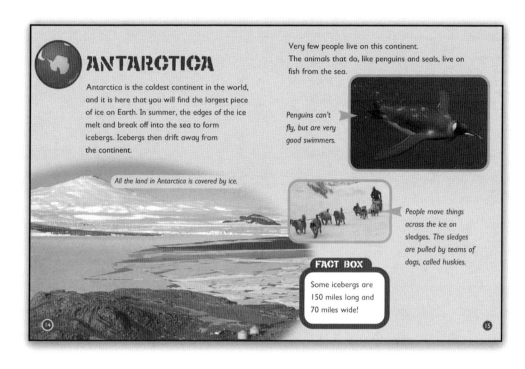

Penguins can't fly, but are very good swimmers.

All the land in Antarctica is covered by ice.

People move things across the ice on sledges. The sledges are pulled by teams of dogs, called huskies.

FACT BOX

Some icebergs are 150 miles long and 70 miles wide!

Read page 16

Purpose: to understand how to use a glossary.

 Pause at page 16

What do you notice about the words in bold?

On what page did you read about poachers / lichen / coral reef?

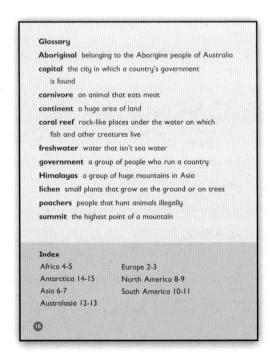